Text copyright © Michael Hardcastle 2001
Illustrations copyright © Dave Thompson 2001
Book copyright © Hodder Wayland 2001

Published in Great Britain in 2001 by Hodder Wayland, an imprint of
Hodder Children's Books

The right of Michael Hardcastle and Dave Thompson to be identified as the
author and illustrator of this Work has been asserted by them in accordance
with the Copyright, Designs and Patents Act 1988.

British Library Cataloguing in Publication Data
(to come)

ISBN: 0 7502 3534 9

Designed by Leishman Design

Printed in Hong Kong by Wing King Tong Co. Ltd

Hodder Children's Books
A division of Hodder Headline Limited
338 Euston Road, London NW1 3BH

Skateboard Secret

MICHAEL HARDCASTLE

Illustrated by Dave Thompson

HODDER
Wayland

an imprint of Hodder Children's Books

Chapter One

Robbie didn't see the danger until the very last moment. Then it was too late to avoid it. He should have heard it but he was lost in his own thoughts. He was coming out of a side-turning when he ran straight into another rider's path. He couldn't even swerve. He had one foot off his deck when the collision happened.

Robbie crashed to the ground but the other boy came off worse. His skateboard took him skittering across the walkway and threw him into a wall. But when the boy picked himself up he was too angry to feel pain. He was examining his board minutely, checking it for the smallest sign of damage. Like his jacket, it was covered in red-and-yellow flashes and looked as if it had seen better days. From where Robbie was standing, however, the board looked perfectly OK.

"Sorry," Robbie muttered, knowing it had been his fault completely. He just hadn't expected anyone else to be in the mall this early. When he was on his own he often rode with his eyes closed. He believed he could get a real feel of the board through his feet that way. This was why he hadn't seen the other skateboarder until a split-second before they had collided.

"What were you trying to do?" the other boy demanded angrily, adding "This is *my* zone, you know."

"I'm just doing a few kickflips and grinds that's all," Robbie replied mildly. "And I always use this place, but I've never seen you here. What's your name?"

"Joe. Go-Joe, that's me. Because I'm always on the move, I'm always on the GO!" said the boy almost fiercely.

"OK," murmured Robbie. "So how good are you when you're on the move, Joe?"

"The best."

Robbie had heard enough. It was time for action. A quick glance at a nearby ramp and he'd sized up the situation. "Watch!" he ordered. He pushed off, pumped up speed towards the ramp, lifted off, spun, spun almost a 360, and came down lightly on the other side, feet firmly in place – and still running. He felt a rush of happiness. He didn't always manage to get air time quite as good as that.

Joe was impressed. There was no doubt about that. Robbie saw his eyes widen. To Robbie's surprise he even admitted it. "Not *bad*," he commented. Robbie wondered whether Joe would now try to show off *his* boarding skills.

"Yeah, well, I can do better than that," Joe said, predictably. But even as he jumped on to his board he misjudged the distance. And as he stumbled off, the board went hurtling across the narrow walkway. With a loud bang it hit a shop door. Both boys held their breath, praying the glass wouldn't break.

It didn't. But light flooded the dark shop and the next moment the door was flying open. "What do you think you're playing at?" yelled an angry voice. The man was tall and scarecrow-thin.

"Sorry," Joe muttered. "Just an accident. I, er, lost control of my board."

"You'd lose more than that if I had my way," the man said. "I've suffered enough damage to my shop through you skateboarders. Reckless maniacs, the lot of you! Well, the police are on their way ..."

"Let's get out of here!" Joe urged Robbie. "Come *on*!" and he grabbed his board.

Robbie didn't hesitate. He picked up his own board and the two boys sprinted madly out of the mall. In the safety of the main street they stopped to listen for the wail of police sirens. All was quiet.

"That guy was just bluffing," Joe said. "He didn't call anybody. Anyway, what was he doing in that shop so early? I bet he was robbing it! Hey, let's go back and catch him at it. We might get a reward!"

Robbie shook his head. "I've got things to do. See ya, Joe."

"Hey, hang on," said Joe. "D'you ride on your own?"

"Mostly," Robbie replied.

"Well, come and meet my mates. You can show 'em your tricks. And watch me in action as well. We've got a great place," said Joe. "You'd be crazy to miss out on it."

Robbie was tempted by the invitation. He still hadn't found a good place to practise. "Yeah, I might," he said. "Tell me the details. By the way, I'm Robbie."

A few moments later, Robbie was on his way home, still not sure whether he'd really want to meet Joe again. He suspected that, one way or another, the other skateboarder could mean trouble.

Chapter Two

A couple of days later, Robbie turned up at West End Park. He soon found the old play area where the skateboarders met. It was an old, empty paddling pool that was no good anymore because two of its sides were cracked. They'd managed to convert it into an oval-shaped course with ramps and a curved climb.

Everyone stopped when Robbie arrived and Joe greeted him with a friendly "Hi!" To his surprise, though, Joe was neither the leader of the gang nor the best skater.

Leo was the one who led the way and told the others what they could and couldn't do. He wore a helmet with flames painted on it and a black denim jacket that looked as if someone had ripped the sleeves off it. He obviously didn't think he needed elbow pads – his bare arms were covered in grazes. There was a girl there too, Ella. When she caught Robbie's glance, he grinned and she smiled back.

Leo's best mate was Harry. Although small, Harry was tough-looking, and he was wearing what Robbie was sure were biker gloves.

"Let's have a go on your board, then," Harry demanded as soon as the introductions were over.

Robbie hesitated. He didn't like lending his precious board to anyone. On the other hand, he didn't want to look mean. "OK," he agreed.

Harry stepped on the deck and almost at once fell off. Robbie felt like laughing but everyone else was quiet. So perhaps Harry was always clumsy. He started a trick, trying to do a pop shove-it but he wasn't moving his feet properly. He just couldn't do it. Then, to Robbie's

15

amazement, he said something to Joe and did a handstand.

As soon as he was balanced with his legs straight up in the air, Joe took Robbie's skateboard and placed it carefully on the soles of Harry's feet. Now Robbie saw why he wore padded gloves. They helped to cushion his hands against the rough concrete. Harry walked in a straight line, keeping the skateboard balanced.

One or two of the boys clapped him. Robbie thought he was just acting the clown.

"That was really cool," he said when Harry slung his board back to him. But it was obvious he didn't really mean it.

The rest of them showed what they could do. Ella was pretty good, but Robbie could see that the others acted as if she wasn't even there. Josh was the worst – everything he tried was a failure. So far as Robbie could tell, lanky Josh had no sense of balance. He fell off every time, almost as soon as his board was moving. Robbie wanted to tell him to bend his knees or go into a crouch. But he didn't know how Josh would take it. He might hate being offered advice by anyone, let alone by a total stranger.

"So what do you think of this place, then?" Joe asked Robbie eagerly.

"Not bad," was Robbie's answer. He didn't really think much of it, but he wasn't going to say so.

"We're going to build a real vert ramp over there, like a ski jump," Joe said, pointing to the far end of the pool. "Harry's big brother says he can get us the stuff to make it. He works for a do-it-yourself place."

"Oh, right," Robbie said in a bored voice. He looked round for Leo and spotted him talking to someone standing on the other side of the fence – a tall, thin boy with floppy hair.

It looked almost as if they were having an argument, with Leo doing most of the arguing. Every time the boy opened his mouth to  speak, Leo put his hands over his ears. It was obvious that he didn't want to listen to anything the other boy had to say.

"Who's that?" he asked Joe, pointing.

"Oh, that's Paul. Wants to ride with us, but Leo doesn't think he's good enough," Joe replied.

This seemed a bit odd to Robbie, when Harry and Josh weren't much good, either. Still, it was nothing to do with him. As Robbie watched, Leo suddenly turned and walked away from the fence. Paul stood staring after him for a moment then shrugged his shoulders and hurriedly walked off towards the park gates.

Robbie turned to pick up his board – but couldn't see it. Maybe somebody had moved or borrowed it? He couldn't see anyone using it.

"My board's missing. It's vanished," he said anxiously to Joe.

Joe's expression didn't change. He looked neither surprised nor upset. Suddenly he announced in a loud voice: "Hey, Robbie here thinks his board's been nicked. Anybody want to own up?"

Robbie was upset. "Hey, I didn't say it had been STOLEN. I just said it was missing!"

Leo was over to them in a flash. "Hey, who're you accusing? Nobody here's a thief!"

Robbie was shaking his head, bewildered at the way things were turning out.

"I didn't say that, Leo, I just said it's missing. And it is. I mean, a minute ago it was here on the ground and now it's gone!"

This time Leo spun round and announced loudly: "Robbie here can't find his board. Anybody got it? If so, own up. Come on!"

They waited in total silence for several moments. No one else said a word or made a move. All the time Robbie was trying to work out what to do next. He felt there would be trouble if he wasn't careful.

"There you are," Leo said triumphantly, "Nobody knows anything. Nobody's got your pathetic board."

"OK," Robbie shrugged. "It's not the end of the world. I mean, I've got another so ..."

"Oh, a rich kid, eh?" said Leo nastily. "Got so many toys to play with it doesn't matter if you lose one, you can just pick up another."

"No, it's not like that," Robbie insisted, wishing he'd never mentioned his other skateboard. "Listen, I'm going. There's no point me staying, now I've nothing to ride."

"You can borrow my board," Harry offered immediately. "You lent me your board, so ..."

"Look, bring your other board next time, OK?" said Joe. "We're sure to have found your first one by then."

Again, Robbie didn't know what to do or say. If he said he wasn't coming again they'd think he'd decided they were a bunch of crooks or something. Then he caught Ella's eye and saw she was smiling at him.

"Yeah, do come back, Robbie," she said. "I'm sure we'll find your board because we'll all look hard for it. There's just been a little mistake, that's all."

"I'll think about it," was as much as he could promise.

Chapter Three

Next evening, Robbie went off to rugby training at Fairhill Sports Centre with Tom from his class. Tom's ambition was to play rugby for England one day and travel all over the world. Robbie wasn't even all that interested in rugby, but he enjoyed the training sessions. They kept him fit for *his* favourite sport – skateboarding.

"You're still not crashing around on that old plank of wood, are you?" Tom asked Robbie as they took a half-time breather.

Robbie sighed. Tom would always be one of those people who thinks his own sport is the only one that matters and that everything else is for wimps. "Look, riding a board, shooting up steep slopes, doing high spins, stuff like that, well it takes *real* skills," Robbie explained, trying to sound convincing. "I mean, anyone can kick a ball around and fight the opposition. I nearly did that yesterday myself."

"Hey, tell me more!" Tom said excitedly. "Didn't know you liked a punch-up. What was it all about?"

"But I didn't *want* a fight. That's why there wasn't one." Robbie explained. Then he told him exactly what had happened with Joe and his mates. To his credit, Tom listened without interrupting once.

"So, I'm not sure what I should do," Robbie concluded. "If I go there again I might lose my other board. They could just be setting me up for some scam."

"You've *got* to go back and get what's yours. You can't let 'em get away with nicking your stuff. Look, Robs, I'll go along with you if you like. I'll be able to sort 'em out, no danger. No bunch of plank pushers could scare *me*."

"Er, I think I should do it on my own," Robbie decided. "I'm sure they'll have found my board, *if* it was lost. If not, well, that's it – I'm finished with them."

Tom was shaking his head fiercely. "Rob. You've got to teach them a lesson. You can't let them treat you like a loser. Let me come. I'll frighten them!"

Robbie didn't like the idea of turning up with a bodyguard. Still, he had to agree with Tom: he couldn't just abandon his board.

"Listen, Tom. Thanks for the offer. You're a real mate," he smiled. "But I think I should face them on my own first. Then, if things go wrong, well, I'll be glad of your, er, support."

Tom shrugged. "Suit yourself, Robs," he muttered.

What would suit me best, Robbie told himself, would be to get my board back and never see any of them again – except maybe Ella. He grinned to himself as he remembered how she'd seemed keen to see him again too.

Chapter Four

"Got any new tricks, then?" Joe asked as he and Robbie made their way towards West End Park a couple of days later.

"Oh, maybe," Robbie replied casually. "I mean, I keep trying out new things and sometimes they work."

"Me too!" said Joe enthusiastically. "You know, I'm going to be World Champion one day. How about that?"

Joe had turned up at the mall that morning, looking for Robbie. He wanted to make sure he was going to come to the park again. Robbie still hadn't decided whether he wanted to meet up with Joe and his mates again. After all, the only one he really liked was Ella. He guessed he wouldn't learn anything new about boarding from them. So he'd decided that although he'd agree to go to the park with Joe he'd leave as soon as he got his board back.

"There is a world champion but he's in America," he told Joe as they went through the park gates. "That's where all the top sports guys are."

"Yeah – and that's where I'm going. Just as soon as I get the dough," Joe replied. "I'll meet the World Champ, I'll watch him, learn all his moves, then take over! I'll knock him out of the contest – wham! You just watch!"

"Well, great," Robbie said. "Hope you make it, Joe."

"I will, you'll see," said Joe. They turned into the park and headed for the old play area. Then Joe stopped dead: "What's happened?" he asked, horror-struck.

"What d'you mean ..." Robbie started to say. Then he saw where Joe was staring.

The area around the paddling pool was
surrounded by a high fence. Barbed wire was
looped all around the top to stop anyone from
climbing over. The pool was piled up with
bricks, breeze blocks, bags and packages of all
kinds of building materials.

Joe sped off fast towards it, leaving Robbie to follow. Even before he reached the wire fence, Robbie saw that Leo had already found a way in. He was stalking around inside, clutching his skateboard, as if he was looking for a space to ride it. But there wasn't any. The building materials were piled simply everywhere.

"Who's done this?" Joe was asking, as if he was still unable to believe his eyes. "I mean, we've got to get rid of this rubbish right away."

"No chance of that," snapped Leo. "This stuff belongs to builders. They've moved in to stay, to build something. They've nicked our skateboard park. Paul is behind this. I know it!" Suddenly, he swung round to glare at Robbie. "Wait a moment. Paul wouldn't have the guts to pull off a stunt like this. This is your stupid trick isn't it?" he said.

Robbie was amazed at the accusation. How could Leo imagine that he had anything at all to do with it? Did he think he could persuade a builder to move onto the site overnight? "What are you talking about Leo? I mean ..."

"You did this to get revenge, didn't you! Because you think *we* nicked your board!" Leo was blazing with anger.

"Don't be stupid ..." Robbie was starting to say when Leo lunged at him and pushed him hard in the chest.

"Don't call *me* stupid, you liar!"Leo was shouting. The push had taken Robbie by surprise. He staggered backwards but just managed to keep his balance.

He was so angry he felt like hitting back at Leo. Joe must have guessed what was going through his mind. He moved forwards and put his hand on Robbie's arm. "Calm down," he said.

Robbie flung off Joe's hand. "It's OK! I'm not going to do anything stupid!" He was glad he hadn't brought Tom with him. By now, Leo would probably be lying unconscious on the ground.

"Listen Leo," Robbie said as calmly as he could manage. "I'm not a liar. I told you, I know nothing about this and I mean it."

"I'm sure Robbie knows nothing about this," said Joe hurriedly. "He was just as surprised as me when we came in and saw all this building stuff."

By now, Harry and Josh had arrived and were watching to see what would happen next. Paul, too, had turned up but, as usual, he stayed on the other side of the fence. Anyway, none of the others was taking any notice of him.

Leo's anger had cooled by now and he was starting to think about the future.

"We've nowhere to go skating now," he said mournfully. "What are we going to do?"

37

Robbie was sympathetic but he wasn't going to get involved. It was their problem. He was still upset about losing his skateboard. "Look, I'm sorry about what's happened here. But before everybody leaves, I would like to know what's happened to my board. Anybody know anything?" he tried.

Leo shook his head. "No idea. Don't care, either. Losing your stupid board isn't as important as losing this place. I built all the ramps, you know. I ..."

"Losing it is important to *me*," Robbie interrupted. "Someone here is a crook!"

He thought Leo would start to say he knew
nothing about it again but he didn't. He just
rubbed each of his bare arms and then turned
towards his friends. They were either staring at
him or poking about among the building blocks.
"Go on, then, tell me who's got this guy's stupid
skateboard," Leo said loudly. "Because when he
gets it back, we'll see the back of him."

"Wasn't me, *you* know that," Joe said at once. "I brought Robbie here. He's a mate. So I wouldn't rob him."

Robbie nodded, accepting Joe's argument. The others, though, remained silent. He looked at Harry who was fiddling with the coloured wheels on his yellow board as if he'd just found something wrong.

"How about you, Harry?" he asked quietly. "I mean, you were the one who rode it. What did you think of it?"

Harry didn't speak for some moments, still playing with the truck. Then he muttered: "Not as good as *this*. I don't want somebody else's junk. No way."

Robbie expected them to rubbish his board because that was their way of telling him to get lost. It didn't bother him. All that mattered was getting it back somehow. He turned to the others. "How about you, Josh?"

"I think you're crazy. Nobody here would steal anything. The only thieves are the guys who've taken our skate park. *They've* stolen from us!" replied Josh.

"OK," Robbie said. He could see that he was going to get nothing useful from anyone.

Then he remembered Ella. He couldn't
believe she would steal from him. "Where's Ella?"
he asked.

"Oh yeah, maybe she's the one who took your
board," Leo suggested immediately. "That's why
she hasn't turned up."

Robbie shook his head. "I don't think she'd do
that. I just wondered where she was. Do you
know where she lives? I mean, she might know
something. She might have seen someone walk
off with it."

"Look," said Leo, "why don't you just go and
find her? Then you can ask her yourself."

Robbie nodded. "Know where she lives?" he
inquired again.

There were mutterings from the others but no one had any real idea. "I think it's somewhere near Stanway Road. Saw her coming out of a house along there once," Joe volunteered. "Oh, yeah, and I saw a name on her board – Luton – something like that. OK?"

"OK," Robbie agreed, ready now to walk away and never see Joe and his mates again. He wouldn't miss them, he'd just ride on his own again in the mall. Then he remembered that Paul had watched everything that happened that time. So he asked the others whether they thought he'd got it.

"No," Leo said hurriedly. "We don't let him near us."

Robbie was puzzled. "But why? He seemed interested enough. Can't he ride or something?"

"No. And he hasn't got his own board," Leo said firmly.

"Oh," Robbie was surprised. "Well, then, that makes him the likeliest person to nick my board. *If* he wants one. Anyone know where he lives? Or his surname?"

"Look, he's not a real skateboarder so just forget him," Leo insisted. Joe nodded in agreement, so Robbie decided to leave it at that.

If he found Ella he could ask her.

Without a backward glance, he left. Joe might try to keep in touch but Robbie didn't want any more to do with him. The incident of the missing board would always come between them even if it turned up.

Robbie went home, collected his bike and set off for the mall. He took his board and protective gear in his back pack. The mall should be empty of shoppers by now and he was certain Joe wouldn't be there.

He steered clear of the shop where Joe had run into trouble. As soon as he was back on familiar ground, Robbie did a few runs with his eyes closed then tried an ollie. It was a brilliant one and he felt happy again. Then he practised spins. His greatest ambition was to turn two complete circles in the air and land perfectly.

He knew he might never do this, but he would never stop trying. His ambition was just as strong as Joe's. He'd be World Champion if he could. That thought was always in his mind when he skated. He *had* to keep mastering new skills because that was what made a true champion stand out.

His second board, the one he was using now, was lighter and not so easy to control. What *had* happened to the first? Robbie hated mysteries. And anyway, why should the thief be allowed to get away with it?

Before he went to bed that night, Robbie studied a local street map. Stanway Road was just off the by-pass and not hard to get to, though he'd need to go by bike.

Next, he worked his way through the letter 'L' in the phone book, but couldn't find any names like 'Luton' listed. But there were several Lawtons and one of them was in Stanway Road – R. Lawton at number 8. That had to be it! Well, it was worth a try – Robbie felt quite excited by what might happen next.

Chapter Five

The next day was Saturday and Robbie set off early on his bike to find Stanway Road. It was in a part of town he'd never been to before. When he got there he found himself in a wide, leafy road. Trees grew at intervals along the pavement and no cars were parked along it because every house had a garage and most had a broad driveway. Number 8 was a big double-fronted house with a circular drive up to the front door and a flower-filled front garden.

At first, Robbie thought he must have the wrong place. Surely Ella didn't live here? And if she did then she must be rich enough to buy a shopful of skateboards. She certainly wouldn't need one or want to steal one. Robbie stood on the pavement for a long time wondering what to do. Should he ring the doorbell? He took a 10p coin from his pocket and spun it in the air: heads 'yes', tails 'no'. It was heads.

He laid down his bike just inside the drive, and
slipped off his back-pack. He'd brought his
skateboard with him. He'd decided that if he
couldn't find Ella he would find somewhere new
to skate instead.

To his relief when he rang the doorbell, Ella herself answered it. She even remembered his name. "Robbie! Hi, what a surprise. What are you doing here?"

"I came to find you," he said, sounding calmer than he felt. "I, er, wanted to see you again. And you weren't at the park yesterday. Nobody knew where you were. What's wrong?"

Before answering, she carefully closed the door behind her and stepped out past Robbie on to the drive.

"It's all a bit embarrassing," she confessed as she led him round the side of the house.

"Why?" He hadn't the faintest idea what she was talking about.

"Well, you see, I knew what was going to happen about our skateboarding place but I couldn't tell Leo and the others," she said, still walking ahead of him. "They might've thought I'd let them down or something. It was best just to let them find out for themselves."

"They did that all right. They were pretty mad about it. Actually, they thought I'd done it, because I blamed them for my missing skateboard."

"What? That's crazy!"

"I know that, but they didn't. I nearly had a fight with Leo about it. I mean, he thinks he'll never get anywhere as good to skate again. So ... how did you know?"

By now they were in the back garden which stretched all the way to a line of tall trees beyond a tennis court. Big enough to have its own skate park, thought Robbie.

Ella sat down on a long garden seat and turned to look at Robbie.

"Well, it's simple, really. My dad's a builder and it's his firm that's doing the development in West End Park," she explained. "He told me about it because he knows I love skateboarding and he'd heard some kids used the old play area for that. But he didn't know that I went there and I didn't tell him. That's why I had to keep clear, Robbie."

Robbie was wondering whether to ask Ella about his missing board. Somehow, though, it didn't seem the right time. Instead, he asked: "So where are you going to skate now? There doesn't seem to be anywhere we can use."

"Well, I've got some great news about that!" Ella exclaimed, her eyes alight with excitement. "Dad has found somewhere for me, somewhere really fantastic. But he doesn't want me to tell everyone because they might invade it." She paused and then rushed on: "But I can tell you, Robbie, because I think we're going to be mates. Do you?"

Robbie thought this was the best thing he'd heard for a long time. "Yeah, I'd like that, Ella. I really would."

"Good! But you've got to promise you won't tell anybody else. We've got to keep this place a secret. Capital letters. S-E-C-R-E-T."

"Promise."

"Right. Did you come on your bike? Have you got your skateboard?" He nodded and Ella continued: "Good. Then we can go there now. You'll be the first person in the world I've shown the secret skate park to. I won't be long. Just got to go and change and pick up my board and gear."

A few minutes later they were heading away from Stanway Road towards the by-pass. Robbie reckoned he must have spent more time riding his bike than his board recently.

At last Ella slowed down, signalled left, and then swung in between twin stone pillars which must have once supported tall gates. A large signboard stood at the top of a drive with the name: 'Grange Hotel' painted on it in ornate letters, followed by a line of four gold stars. A notice was also stuck across the board: a white banner with just one word in red: CLOSED.

Ella carried on until she'd gone all the way past the front of the hotel, through a side yard crowded with skips and dustbins, and on to a cracked terrace at the back of the hotel. She skidded to a halt in front of a large swimming pool with a pale-blue floor. It was easy to see the bright colour because there wasn't a single drop of water in it.

"Well, what d'you think?" Ella demanded excitedly. "Isn't it a fantastic place for skating? I mean, look at that slope up towards the shallow end. That's just the perfect take-off ramp."

Robbie nodded. It was true. He could begin to imagine how, with a couple of ramps and maybe some fun boxes, it would be ideal. A metal ladder led halfway to the floor at the deep end, so it would be easy to get down into the pool.

"Fantastic!" he nodded. "But what about the owners? They'll go mad if we start skateboarding here. They ..."

"No they won't," Ella grinned. "That's the best thing about all this. Dad's firm owns the hotel now and they're going to turn it into a leisure centre or something. But until they do we can use it whenever we like. Dad said I can bring along who I like as long as it's not too many. So long as George, the security guy, knows. He keeps an eye on the place when the builders aren't here. Look, that's him over there. Hi George!" Ella waved to a tall man in a security guard's uniform who'd been watching them from the hotel. He waved back and gave Ella the thumbs up sign.

"So, how would you like to have a go now?" went on Ella.

"Great!" Robbie said eagerly. "Good thing I decided to bring my board with me today."

Moments later they were down on the pool floor. "It's really good to be here riding with someone else," Ella said as they pumped up speed side by side.

Robbie started doing tricks, jumping and twisting time and again, trying to manage a complete circle before landing on the run. At last he managed it. Ella had stopped riding to watch him and she clapped loudly when he finally made it. "I'm going to have a go now," she announced. "So watch me, Robbie, and tell me if I'm getting it wrong."

She was good, though Robbie thought her board was too light for that particular trick. "Try to get higher on your jump," he told her. "The higher you get the more likely it'll work. Go on, *force* yourself upwards."

It took her another dozen goes before she succeeded, but then she did it again. "You're a fast learner, Ella," Robbie told her. After that they competed against each other in speed runs and tic-tacs before Ella said they ought to go home.

"So you'll come again?" she asked Robbie as they cycled back towards her house.

"Just try and stop me," he replied. "Best skate park I've ever used. And we can make it even better if we fix up a few jumps and things – or, er, your dad fixes 'em for us!"

"He will. Listen, I'd like to ask Paul to come along. Know who I mean? He used to come to West End Park when we were there but Leo wouldn't let him join in. He said he was a hopeless skater and wouldn't fit in!"

Robbie didn't know quite what to say about Paul. He hardly knew him anyway so all he said was: "Sure."

"Right, we'll drop in now and give him the good news," Ella decided.

Paul lived in a small end-of-terrace house on a road that sloped steeply down towards the town centre. And as they turned into the road they saw Paul making good use of the slope. He was riding confidently down it at top speed. It didn't take Robbie a second to recognize *what* he was riding.

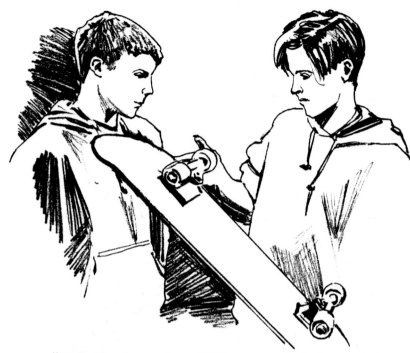

"Hey, that's my board," he gasped. "Where did you get it?"

"Found it," replied Paul, looking surprised. "Why? D'you want it back?"

"Course I do! It's my best board. I was using it at West End Park when it was nicked."

"Well, it wasn't me. I found it in the bushes. Thought it had been thrown away."

"I expect Leo or one of that lot chucked it there for a joke," Ella suggested, anxious to prevent a row between Robbie and Paul.

"Yeah, I suppose so. It'd be just like them," Paul agreed. "Sorry, Robbie. Here, take it back."

"Don't you have a board?" Robbie asked.

"Yeah, of course. I was just using yours for extra practice. It's pretty good."

With that now out of the way, Ella told Paul about her secret skateboard park and invited him to come along.

"It sounds brilliant," Paul said. He paused and then added: "Do you mind if I bring somebody with me?"

Ella was surprised. But she said: "Yes, of course. Who?"

"Leo."

"Leo!" Robbie and Ella exclaimed. How could Paul want to be friends with him?

"Well, he's my step-brother now, you see," Paul explained, turning pink. "We don't get on all that well yet, but I want us to. So this could help. Also, Leo's got nowhere to skate, so your new place would be perfect."

Ella glanced at Robbie. "What do you think, Robs?"

Robbie blinked. "It's your place, Ella," he said. "So you decide."

"Right," she announced. "Leo can come. But no stupid stuff or we'll throw him out. You tell him that, Paul."

"I will. Thanks Ella!"

They arranged to meet at the hotel pool the next day. Then Robbie set off home, carrying the skateboard he thought he'd lost for ever. He kept wondering what would happen when he met Leo again. Had he and Ella done the right thing letting him share their secret skateboard park? But then, maybe Leo wouldn't want to have anything to do with Robbie ever again.

Chapter Six

When Robbie and Ella arrived at the hotel pool the next day, Paul and Leo were waiting for them. Leo grinned and said: "Great place, this. Now I'll be able to show you I'm a true champ. Only the best place will do for the best guy, you know."

Then he lowered his voice and said hurriedly: "Look, Robbie. Sorry about the stupid skateboard scam. It was Joe's idea and we all went along with it. We do it to everyone who wants to join the gang. It's a sort of test. Paul had nothing to do with it, honest."

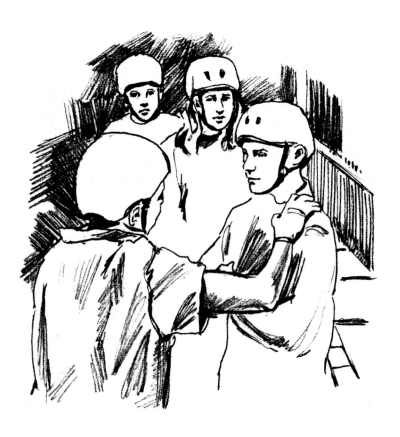

Robbie felt the anger rising up in him: "Yeah, well it *was* stupid. You know you're only here because Paul insisted..."

"Maybe we should just *all* forget about it now," interrupted Ella. "This is my place, so what *I* say goes! Anyway, Robbie's got some tricks you've never even heard of, Leo."

They performed the best tricks they knew. It was if they were all competing in the world championships or something. Robbie was a whirl of wheels and wood and even managed a one-hand stand for a few seconds before bouncing into the pool wall.

Ella and Leo managed some impressive
jumps, but neither of them could match Paul.
He could do the most amazing flips and spins.
He was so impressive, the others stopped skating
and stood watching him.

At one point, Paul even managed a grab –
holding his deck in mid-air to turn the board as
he landed. Robbie had performed that a couple
of times, but he'd never tried it in front of other
skaters in case he made a mess of it. But Paul
was full of confidence, or perhaps it was that he
wanted to show his step-brother just how good
he was. Maybe if they liked the same sport they'd
get on better.

"Hey, I never guessed you could do tricks like that, Paul. You're brilliant," Robbie said seriously.

Paul glanced round before whispering. "Well, that's why Leo didn't want me at West End Park. I'm better than him."

Robbie nodded. Suddenly, Paul froze and Robbie looked down, embarassed. Leo was closer to them than they'd realised and it was obvious he'd overheard. But Leo was grinning.

"Listen, brother," he said, smiling as he spoke. "You and Robs might be the best at the moment.

But I'm going to beat you both out of sight because I never stop aiming for the top, OK?"

"OK!" said Paul happily.

"Sure you will, Leo," Robbie said smoothly. "Sure you will." But he was smiling too.

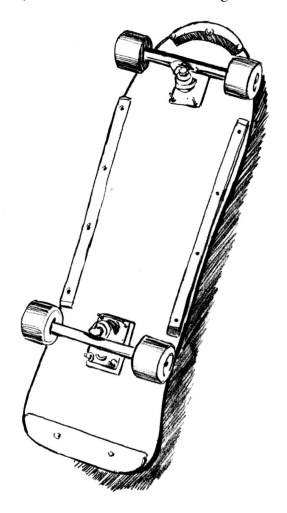

Read more of Michael Hardcastle's sports stories:

INJURY TIME
Joe would be a really good player, if he weren't so accident prone. He always seems to be suffering from aches and pains and rarely gets through a match without injury. The coach thinks that he's a fake, but Amy's not sure. Could there be another reason for Joe's problem?

STRIKER'S BOOTS
Sean has waited for weeks to get a place on the school soccer team. He's almost given up hope when the coach picks him at last! Then disaster strikes. He's forgotten his boots. This could be Sean's big chance, but how can he score goals in bare feet?

SOCCER SECRET
Tom is a brilliant striker and he loves boasting about all the goals he scores. But he doesn't know that his cousin Alan is good at football too - as a goalie. Will Alan get the recognition he deserves, without upsetting Tom?

RIVALS UNITED
When East End's star striker defects to the West End team, his team-mates can't believe it. Just what does David think he's playing at? Then there's a local derby when the two teams meet. The winning team could be promoted to league status, but where do David's loyalties lie?

DOWNHILL BIKER

Aaron and Dean are deadly rivals for the Three Peaks Race and both are tipped to win. When Aaron damages his bike, his chances of beating Dean on his gleaming new machine start to fade. Just when things can't get any worse Aaron's bike goes missing. Will it turn up in time for the race?

For more information about Mega Stars, please contact: The Sales Department, Hodder Children's Books, 338 Euston Road, London NW1 3BH